Alex Spiro and Sam Arthur would like to thank Robert Ipcar for his invaluable assistance with this project and Dahlov Ipcar for her beautiful words and pictures and for the honour to introduce them to a new generation of children.

We would also like to thank the Nobrow design team for their meticulous labour on the restoration of the artwork to its original form.

I Like Animals

Dahlov Ipcar

FLYING EYE BOOKS

This is a first Flying Eye Books edition.
I Like Animals is © 2014 Flying Eye Books.
First published as a Borzoi Book by Alfred A. Knopf Inc. in 1960.

Published by Flying Eye Books, an imprint of Nobrow Ltd.
62 Great Eastern Street, London, EC2A 3QR.

ISBN 978-1-909263-25-3

Order from www.flyingeyebooks.com

I like animals. All kinds of animals. little ones, big ones.

Plain ones, strange ones,

Bright red ladybugs,

and green grasshoppers,

hefty hippos and wrinkled rhinos.

I like peacocks and ocelots.

I like sparrows and alley cats.

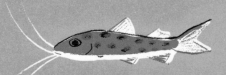

I like starfish

and jellyfish

and catfish.

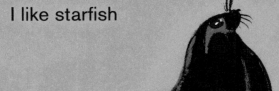

I like smooth, wet, shining seals.
I like big, rough, shaggy buffaloes.
I like anything alive, flying, crawling, walking, swimming,

bullfrogs hopping

spiders spinning

hummingbirds humming

butterflies fluttering

snails sliding

earthworms wriggling

penguins diving

I like animals.

I wish I were a keeper in a great big zoo – with elephants and camels and ponies to ride.

I'd have a cage full of pelicans and toucans and flamingos, macaws and cockatoos and birds of paradise.

There'd be zebras and giraffes and bongos and gemsbok and kudus and okapis,
and all kinds of antelope from the plains of Africa grazing on the grass.

There'd be snakes in a snake house, and monkeys in a monkey house – gorillas and orangutans and chimpanzees, too. There'd be cages full of animals from far off places: kangaroos and pandas and ostriches and anteaters.

I'd have lions in a lion den and bears in a bear den, and tigers pacing and leopards snarling. There'd be sea lions barking and diving in their pool.
I wish I were the keeper in a zoo.

I wish I had a pet shop full of all kinds of pets – with a window full of puppies and kittens and pigeons. There'd be pussycats purring and puppies' tails wagging.

I'd have cages and cages full of bright birds singing and big tanks full of fancy
fish swimming.

I'd have all kinds of puppies:

Poodles and

Pekinese

Bulldogs

and Basset hounds

Danes and

Dalmatians

Dachshunds

and Dobermans

I'd have pens full of guinea pigs and rabbits and mice: black ones, white ones, spotted, and Dutch-belted ones. There'd be rabbits with long ears and noses that wiggle, and little golden hamsters with shining black eyes.

I'd have goldfish and angelfish and Siamese fighting fish,

little green turtles and bright red snails.

I might even have some monkeys

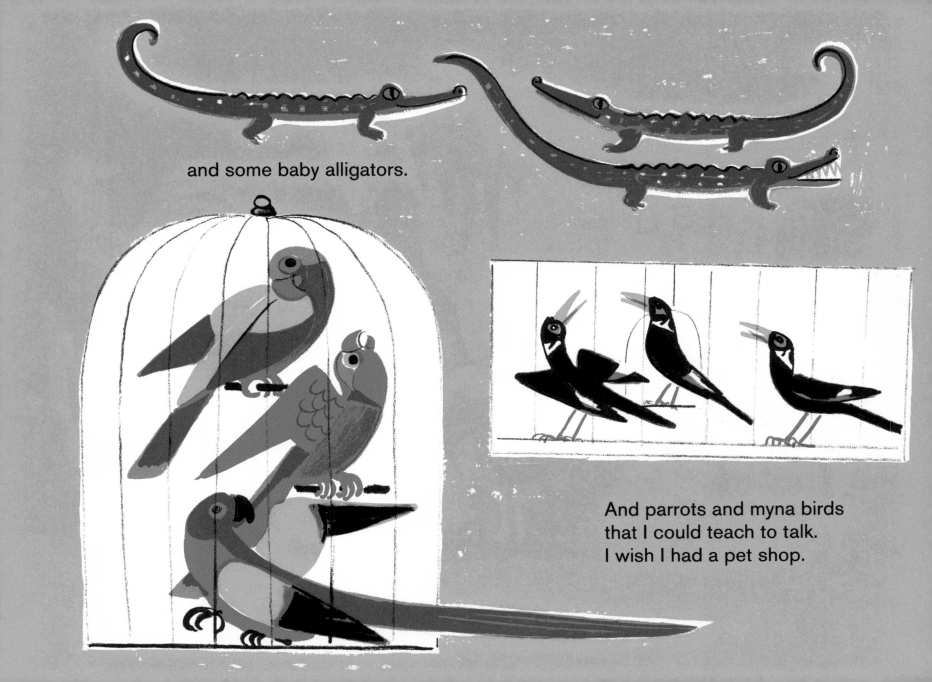

and some baby alligators.

And parrots and myna birds
that I could teach to talk.
I wish I had a pet shop.

I wish I were a farmer with a big green farm – with a big tractor and a great big barn. I wish I had a barnyard full of all kinds of animals:

sheep and pigs and chickens and ducks and geese, goats and horses and ponies and turkeys and guinea hens, Guernsey cows, Jersey cows, Holsteins, and Dutch-belted cows.

There'd be mares with their little colts running in the meadows. There'd be big sows grunting and baby piglets squealing and big sheep baaing and baby lambs blatting.

There'd be big cows mooing and baby calves maaing. Big rooster crowing and
fat hens clucking with their little chicks peeping and scratching in the dirt.

There'd be a big golden collie dog to bring home the cows. There'd be pussycats and pigeons and swallows in the barn. There'd be every kind of farm animal on my farm.

I wish I were a farmer.

I wish I were a woodsman living in a cabin deep in the woods – with big black bears coming to visit me, and raccoons and porcupines living in the trees. I'd watch gray squirrels and little striped chipmunks chasing up and down the tree trunks, and butterflies flitting through the patches of sunlight.

I'd see woodcocks, and partridges eating red berries. There'd be striped skunks, and foxes, and shy deer hiding, and flying squirrels gliding high overhead.

I'd hear wild wolves howling and bobcats yowling and big owls hooting,
"Whooo…hoo!" in the night-time. But, I'd be sleeping safe inside my log cabin.

In the morning, I'd hear wild birds singing, blue jays crying and woodpeckers hammering, high in the treetops all around me. There'd be little frogs croaking in the forest pool, and I'd watch the deer and the big moose coming down to drink.

I wish I were a woodsman.

When I grow up, I'll have a zoo or a pet shop.

When I grow up, I'll be a farmer or a woodsman.

But right now I only have five goldfish and two turtles, a beagle and a boxer and three cats, a salamander and a parakeet, and a jar full of ants that I dug up in the yard. And I have a frog that I caught, and a June bug, and a waltzing mouse named Yo-yo. I have to feed them and take care of them all. But I wish I had lots more animals
BECAUSE I LIKE ANIMALS.